AF606900

MONSTER MACHINES

ANTONOV 124 CARGO PLANE

John Bankston

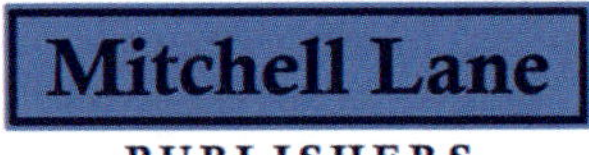

2001 SW 31st Avenue
Hallandale, FL 33009
www.mitchelllane.com

First Edition, 2020.

Author: John Bankston
Designer: Ed Morgan
Editor: Lisa Petrillo

Little Mitchie is an imprint of Mitchell Lane Publishers.

Names/credits:
Title: Antonov 124 Cargo Plane / by John Bankston
Description: Hallandale, FL :
Mitchell Lane Publishers, [2020]

Series: Monster Machines
Library bound ISBN: 9781680204506
eBook ISBN: 9781680204513

Photo credits: Freepik.com, Shutterstock, Cover: TseRonnie CC-BY-SA-3.0, p. 5 Eric Prado CC-BY-SA-3.0, p. 6 Masakatsu Ukon CC-BY-SA-2.0, p. 17 Steve Lynes CC-BY-SA-2.0, p. 18 John Murphy CC-BY-SA-2.0, p. 19 Alert5 CC-BY-SA-4.0,

Contents

Chapter 1

One Powerful Plane

Imagine a plane strong enough to lift the weight of more than 11 African elephants. Eight city buses lined up end-to-end barely stretch the length of its wings. It's almost 70 feet high at the tail.

Heading down a Portland, Oregon runway and bound for Canada, this Antonov 124 is carrying two massive Columbia Helicopters.

This is the Antonov 124. It weighs nearly 400 **tons**. Even though it is so heavy it can still fly while carrying 150 tons of cargo.

There are many huge planes that have been designed, built and fly easily through the skies. Only the Antonov 124 is large and strong enough to carry engines for a Boeing 787 Dreamliner. The Boeing 787 is almost 225 feet long. It weighs almost 300,000 pounds. The body is built in Washington state. The engines are made in Ohio. Bringing the parts together is tough. Train travel takes days. The company could miss delivery dates. Workers could be **idled**. Both would lose money.

In 2016, five jet engines for the Boeing 787 were loaded onto the Antonov 124. That year, the cargo plane also toted a 767 wing from West Palm Beach, Florida.

Boeing 787

The plane is owned by Russia's Volga-Dnepr company. Boeing and Volga-Dnepr are rivals. So are the U.S. and Russia. Yet with this plane rivalries and enemy status seem different. As A. Oakley Brooks, president of the National Air Carriers Association, told a reporter for the *Dayton Daily News*, "They even haul things for the U.S. military." The Antonov 124 has carried tanks, Apache helicopters, and troops. In 2012, it carried a 45-ton railroad car from Germany to India. Loading required railroad tracks running from runway to the cargo hold.

The Antonov 124 uses four powerful jet engines. It was created by a man whose first aircraft used just wind and wings.

FAST FACT

The Antonov 124 has carried a 300-pound locomotive, Boeing Chinook helicopters (three at a time), and yachts for the America's Cup sailing races.

Chapter 2

Flight Dreams

Every other June, airplane fans visit Paris. The city's air show is the oldest in the world, dating back to the start of the 20th century. In 1985, visitors weren't excited by the fastest plane. They lined up for the biggest.

Wearing an American flag pin, Russian flight engineer Antonov Boulanenko showed off the Antonov 124. It was one of Oleg Antonov's last planes.

Antonov 124 at the Paris Air Show in 1985

His first aircraft didn't even have an engine. It was a glider.

Antonov was born in the Soviet Union, where Russia is today. It was a place with many rules and few freedoms under a then-powerful Communist government. In 1938, a flight instructor escaped the country in a glider. The government closed Antonov's factory.

In 1939, Nazi Germany invaded Poland, one of the primary actions that started World War II. The Soviet Union joined England, France, and the United States to fight them as part of the Allied forces. Antonov designed fighters for air attacks for the Allies. The Allies won the war in 1945.

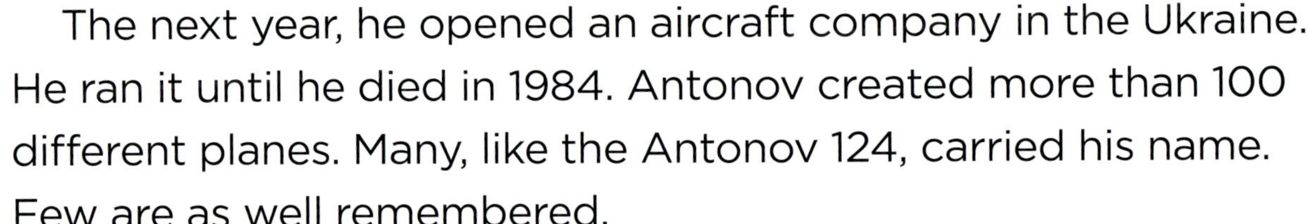

The next year, he opened an aircraft company in the Ukraine. He ran it until he died in 1984. Antonov created more than 100 different planes. Many, like the Antonov 124, carried his name. Few are as well remembered.

It was built to carry Soviet tanks and helicopters. The government wanted it to stand out. It was the biggest plane in the world. "An ordinary company could not build such aircraft," former Russian test pilot Valeriy V. Migunov told a *The New York Times* reporter in 2014.

It would be called the *Russlan*, after a Russian knight. It was nicknamed, "Condor."

The first flying prototype of the Antonov 124 during the loading test at Sheremetyevo airport, Moscow, USSR in March 1986.

FAST FACT

In 1942, Oleg Antonov attached wings and a tail to a 13,000-pound T-60 light tank as a warplane. His experiment with the "flying tank" didn't fly.

Chapter 3

Hard Landings

After a hurricane hit the Gulf Coast in 2005, the Antonov 124 saved lives. The plane delivered a water pump to New Orleans, Louisiana. In 2017, it delivered generators to the French-controlled Guadalupe in the Caribbean after a hurricane.

On approach, the Antonov 124 dwarfs other planes. Although it needs a lot of space, it can handle very rough runways.

Hurricanes can be powerful enough to damage runways. The 124 can land where other planes cannot. Its landing gear has 24 wheels to handle its weight. It is so versatile it can land on hard-packed snow or ice-covered swamps. "Russia, China, and Kazakhstan have a lot of not-so-good airfields," Antonov project manager Viktor N. Kazurov told a reporter for the *New York Times* in 2014.

It can fly when the air temperature is below zero Fahrenheit. It can also handle extreme heat. It's been used to rescue **refugees**. It has carried troops and aid workers. It even helped search for a submarine.

In 2017, an Argentine Navy sub named the ARA San Juan sank off the coast of Argentina. Rescue workers from around the world responded. Onboard an Antonov 124, a team of deep-sea divers, the team commander, and a doctor traveled with a special underwater vehicle called the Pantera Plus. The Pantera remote-controlled deep-sea vehicle played an important part in the search.

Gear of the Russian navy is unloaded from the Antonov 124-100 airplane to take part in the search and rescue mission of the missing Argentine submarine ARA San Juan and its 44 crew members on November 25, 2017.

The Antonov 124 doesn't just fly people or cargo. In the 1990s, it carried a giraffe between two Australian zoos. Air pressure changes as planes climb. The animal could get very sick if it changed too quickly. The Antonov 124 slowly climbed. The giraffe arrived healthy.

FAST FACT

Although the Antonov 124 plane can carry up to 360 soldiers, in 1990 it was used to rescue 451 Bangladeshi refugees.

Chapter 4

How it Flies

Igor Sikorsky made such an impact on airplane engineering that he transformed the design of airplanes far into the future. Early plane designs once used only one engine. During World War I, he created a bomber. To increase the numbers of bombs the plane could carry, Sikorsky used four engines. He kept them close to the **fuselage**. If two engines on one side failed, the plane would become unbalanced and spin. With the engines close together, the pilot could control this.

Lifting into the air, this Antonov 124 reveals its unique landing gear.

The Antonov 124 also has four engines. Its jets burn fuel and turn it into gas. Gas escapes through an opening in the back of the engine. This action creates an opposite reaction—**thrust**. The plane moves.

Inside the 124's engines are two fans. They turn like **propellers**. This increases power and reduces the need for fuel. Still, a 124 carries enough fuel to fill the tanks of 5,000 cars. As the plane speeds down a runway, it achieves lift.

Probably its best feature is the **nose**. In under seven minutes, it can be raised. The back takes less than three minutes. Because a ramp lowered from the cargo hold would be very steep, the plane is able to tip forward to handle loading. It kneels. Wheels below its nose are removed and two "feet" are extended below. Tanks can be driven in the front before takeoff and the back after landing. It also has its own crane, which can lift up to 30 tons.

FAST FACT

In 2016, China's Y-20 entered service. Nicknamed "Chubby Girl," it can only handle half the payload of an Antonov 124. Alongside the U.S. and Russia, China became the third country in the world to design and build its own cargo planes.

Chapter 5

Powerlifter

The Antonov 124 has broken not just one or two world records. It has broken 30 of them. To prove how strong it was, in 1985 it took off with almost 378,000 pounds of cargo. It then flew to 35,269 feet.

The plane could cross the world. In 1987, it flew 12,521 miles in just over one day's time. It didn't have to stop for gas.

In the 1990s, the Antonov began hauling cargo for companies. It carried a Siemens Company power plant generator in 1993 that weighed more than 140 tons. It was the heaviest cargo load ever carried for a company. The next year, it carried cargo that was almost ten tons heavier.

For thirty years, it was the heaviest cargo plane in the world. Today it is still the heaviest plane in regular use.

FAST FACT

The Antonov 124 has a bigger brother. The Antonov 225 was built to carry the Russian Space shuttle, Buran. Its top takeoff weight is over 660 tons. It began flying in 1989. It has six engines and was bigger by half than any other plane. Few companies hire it, because they don't need such a big plane that costs more than $30,000 an hour.

Map

The Antonov 124 is made in Ulianovsk, Russia.

Specs

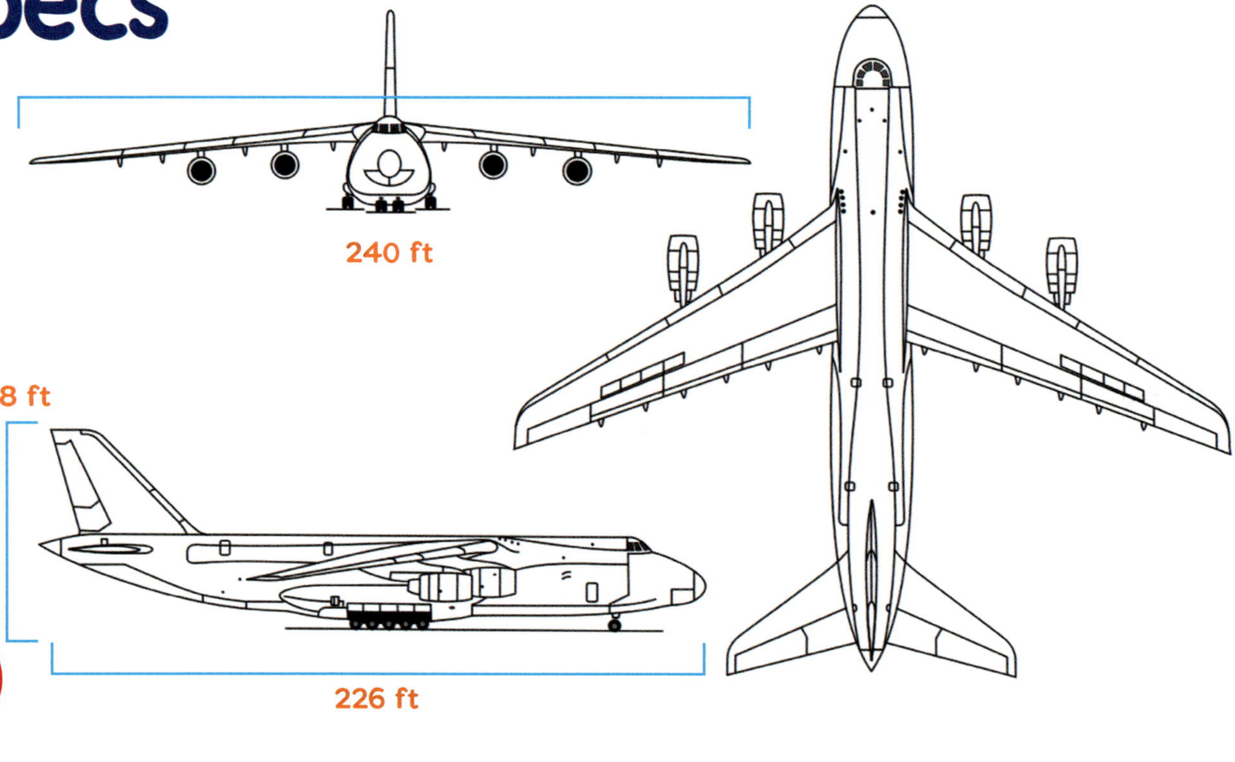

240 ft

68 ft

226 ft

What You Should Know

- Before the Antonov 124, the C-5 Galaxy was the biggest plane on the planet. The C-5 only handles cargo for the U.S. military.
- No other plane its size can be loaded as quickly. In the front, the plane's nose can lift up as if it is on a hinge. To the rear is a door that lowers into a ramp. Cargo can be driven in the front and out the back.
- The fuselage has two levels: top for crew, bottom for cargo.
- The plane flies so high the passengers have to carry oxygen because the air becomes so thin.
- Despite its size, it can take off on a shorter runway than smaller planes.
- It can land on frozen fields and damaged runways.

Glossary

fuselage
The body of a plane

idle
Not working, not active

nose
The front of a plane

propellers
Angled blades that spin and propel a ship or plane

refugees
People forced to flee their country, usually because of war

thrust
The force from a jet engine that lets it move forward quickly

ton
Two-thousand pounds

Find Out More

Goldish, Meish. *Freaky-big Airplanes*. New York, N.Y: Bearport. 2010.

Hayes, Amy. *How a Plane is Made.* New York: Gareth Stevens 2016.

Legendre, Philippe. *Planes, Trains & Moving Machines*. Irvine, CA: Walter Foster Jr., 2015.

White, Rowland, *Cleared for Takeoff: the Ultimate Book of Flight.* San Francisco: Chronicle Books. 2016

On the Internet

Basic facts about airplanes:
http://www.sciencekids.co.nz/sciencefacts/vehicles/airplanes.html
http://www.sciencekids.co.nz/sciencefacts/flight.html

Some Flying History:
http://www.scienceforkidsclub.com/airplanes.html
http://www.scienceshorts.com/cool-facts-airplanes-kids/

Index

About the Author

I've ridden in small private prop planes, giant 747s, and flown in just about everything in between. Yet during the flight, I always have the same question. How is this thing staying in the air? For me, answering that question about one of the world's heaviest planes was very interesting. I loved reading about the progress from single-engine bi-planes to the massive Antonov 124 and the even bigger Antonov 225.